D0452011

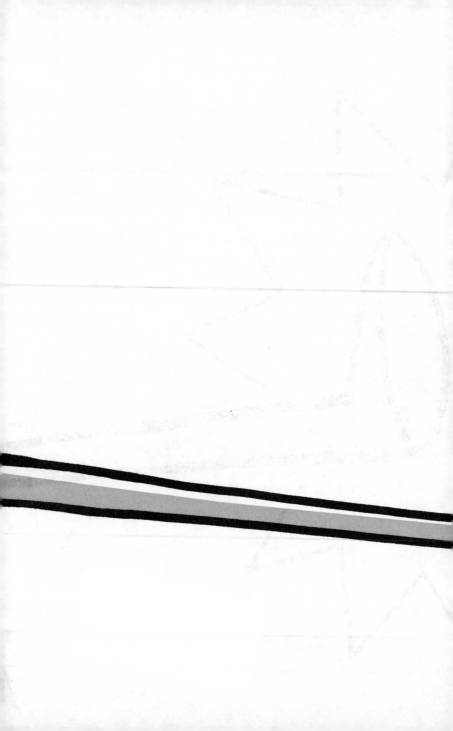

The GUMAZING GUM GIRL! POPPED STAR

RHODE MONTIJO

with Luke Reynolds

BOOK 3

DISNEP • HYPERION
LOS ANGELES   NEW YORK

If you purchased this book without a cover, you should be aware that this book is stolen property. It was reported as "unsold and destroyed" to the publisher, and neither the author nor the publisher has received any payment for this "stripped" book.

Text and illustrations copyright © 2018 by Rhode Montijo

All rights reserved. Published by Disney • Hyperion, an imprint of Disney Book Group. No part of this book may be reproduced or transmitted in any form or by any means, electronic or mechanical, including photocopying, recording, or by any information storage and retrieval system, without written permission from the publisher. For information address Disney • Hyperion, 125 West End Avenue, New York, New York 10023.

First Hardcover Edition, April 2018
First Paperback Edition, April 2019
1 3 5 7 9 10 8 6 4 2
FAC-038091-19060
Printed in the United States of America

This book is set in 12.6-pt. Grilled Cheese BTN Condensed/Fontbros.com
Designed by Maria Elias
Coloring by Joe To

Library of Congress Control Number for Hardcover: 2017046141

ISBN 978-1-4231-6138-7

Visit www.DisneyBooks.com

SUSTAINABLE FORESTRY INITIATIVE

Certified Sourcing
www.sfiprogram.org
SFI-00993

Logo Applies to Text Stock Only

For Floyd Nordwick,
my high school art teacher, who believed in me.

CONTENTS

CHAPTER I

NOTHING BUT
THE TOOTH

LAST TIME . . . Gum Girl had done
the impossible . . . again! Our gumazing heroine
rescued Natalie Gooch, the school bully, from a
raging rhino . . .

. . . AND Gum Girl saved the town from the menacing Robo Chef.

All that superhero work had stretched Gum
Girl to her limit. And now Gabby Gomez was
EXHAUSTED. But she had one more important
thing to do. . . .

Gabby ran toward her *papi*'s dentist office. It
was time she finally told her family the truth
about her secret identity. (And get that aching
tooth checked out, too!)

"¡Aí, sí, mija! It's just as I feared. You have a cavity," Dr. Gomez told Gabby. "I'll need to numb the area. Then I can fill the cavity."

Gabby took a deep breath.

This was her chance.

"Just a minute, *mija*." Dr. Gomez wheeled around in his chair. He readied a shot for Gabby's tooth. Gabby braced for the needle.

"I heard that Gum Girl tackled a robot today!" Dr. Gomez said as he gave Gabby the shot. "I wish her good deeds weren't from chewing gum! All that sugar is so bad for kids' teeth!"

A tingly numbness spread across Gabby's mouth.

A dribble of drool rolled down her chin.

Dr. Gomez kept talking. "Even Rico tried to imitate Gum Girl the other day. What a mess! This could be a dentistry disaster for kids everywhere! Aí, what can we do?"

Dr. Gomez stopped himself. "Oh, I'm sorry, *mija*. What did you want to tell me?"

It was now or never.

Gabby's words were slurred, but her heart was steady.

"What did you say, honey?"

Gabby tried again. "I um hum hirl!"

Dr. Gomez nodded thoughtfully. "Hmm, very interesting."

Gabby continued, "I unted ew el ew a wong wong ime ao."

"I see," Dr. Gomez said, tilting his head to the side while studying her mouth.

Gabby kept going. "I ant eep it uh ekret anemur! I um hum hirl."

Dr. Gomez paused and looked deep into Gabby's eyes. "*Está bien, yo entiendo, mija.* It's okay, I understand that you're nervous, but I appreciate you telling me about it."

Dr. Gomez was suddenly very quiet. Gabby worried that he was mad or sad or maybe mad *and* sad.

The sound of Dr. Gomez's drill suddenly filled the room.

WHIRRR

RRRRRRRRR!

Dr. Gomez drilled.
Dr. Gomez filled.

Then he drilled and filled some more.
At last he finished. Gabby held her breath
waiting for him to say something.

Dr. Gomez leaned back in his chair and breathed a sigh of relief. "I'm so proud of you, Gabriella," he said.

"You are very brave, you know that?" Dr. Gomez winked at Gabby.

Gabby sprang up in her seat and breathed an even louder sigh of relief. Revealing her secret identity had gone *so much* better than she expected.

"You know what I think?" Dr. Gomez said. Before Gabby could speak, he answered his own question. "I need to discuss this with your mom, but I think we should have you try sugarless gum. How does that sound?"

How does that sound? It sounds perfect, Gabby thought. If Papi could take her Gum Girl news so well, then Gabby could switch to sugarless gum. No problem! Nothing could pop her excitement now. Not even sugarless gum.

"D'at hounds ate!" Gabby leaped out of the chair and gave her dad a huge hug.

Dr. Gomez laughed and hugged her back.

"Your mouth may swell, *mija*. Give it time to get back to normal. Okay?"

Gabby laughed, and her heart swelled more than her mouth ever could.

15

CHAPTER 2

FREE TO BE
SUGAR-FREE

Gabby was as light as a balloon. She floated toward home, strolling past the downtown store windows. Gabby tested out her new name. "SUGAR-FREE Gum Girl!" *Hmm.* Not that catchy, but maybe it wouldn't be so bad.

Gabby started to imagine new sugarless gum flavors she might try.

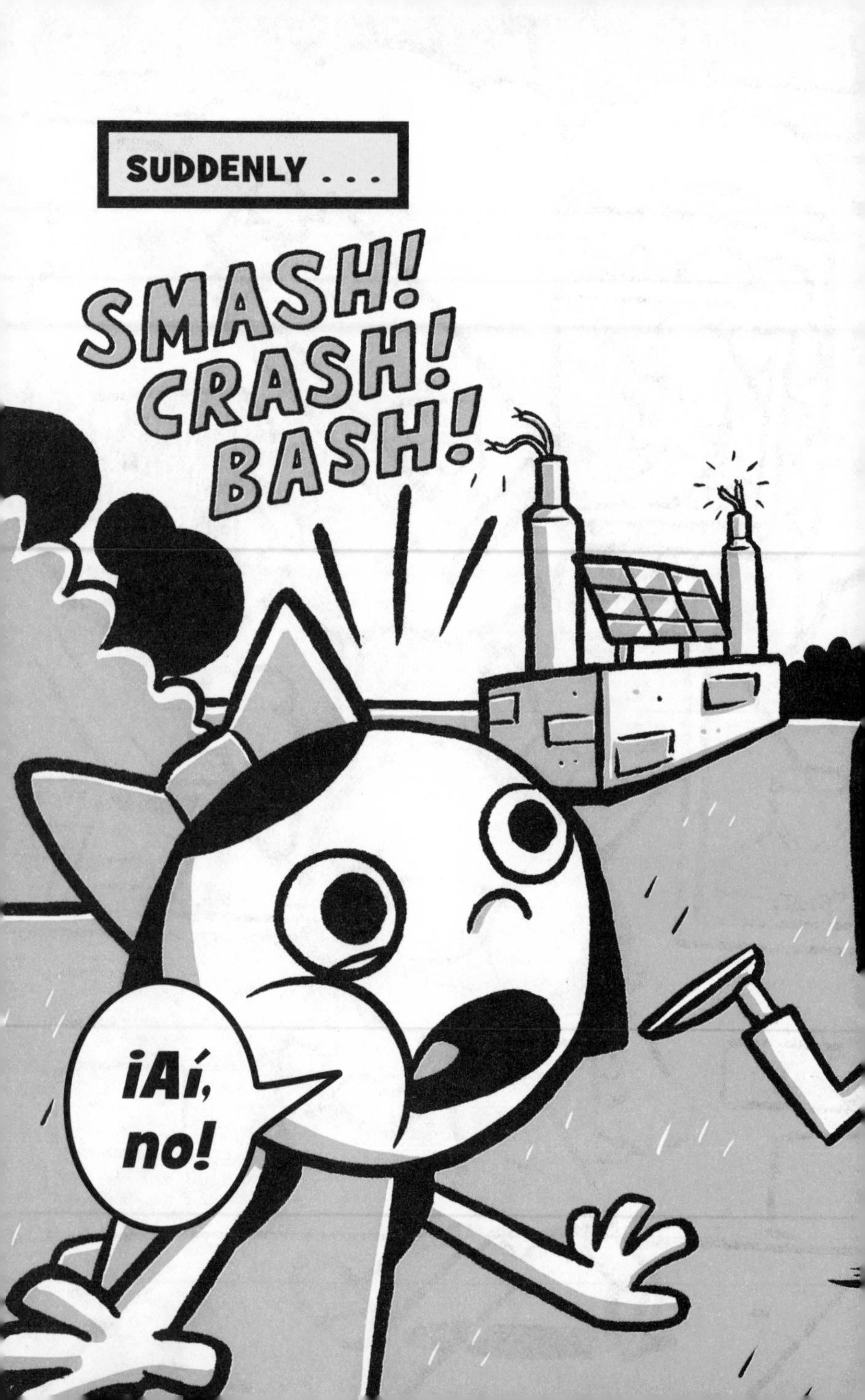
SUDDENLY . . .
SMASH! CRASH! BASH!
¡Aí, no!

Gabby popped out of her daydream. Someone was taking the city's brand-new, solar-powered, digitally enhanced welcome sign!

Think fast! Think fast! Gabby searched around for some gum.

They were getting away with the sign!

WELCOME
POP. 307,072.5

AH!

OUT OF NOWHERE . . .

A figure spun and twirled onto the scene.

"No crime is **TUTU** big for **NINJA-RINA!**" she roared with a gleaming smile.

A masked ballerina jumped into the air, twisted in a full circle, then kicked the sign free.

She swirled, she twirled, she unfurled.
    She looped, she swooped, she booped!

She pranced, she danced, she put those thieves in a trance!

Gabby couldn't believe her eyes. The sign was back where it belonged, and the masked figure—Ninja-Rina—was flipping, fleeing the scene.

Luckily, a camera crew had caught the whole thing on film. One of the crew ran up to Gabby and asked, "Can you describe what just happened here?"

Gabby's face was still swollen, but she tried her best.

"It uz a beeg oblum and sum roobers wuur seeling the shine!"

The woman gave Gabby a funny look, then turned toward the camera. "Well, you saw it here first: another major crime stopped in its tracks! The city's sign is safe, thanks to . . . NINJA-RINA!"

Gabby was glad the sign was safe.

But something felt *tutu* strange. . . .

CHAPTER 3

PRETENDING
TO BE . . . ME?

Gabby's mom and dad were all smiles at dinner.

"Your *papi* told me what you talked about, Gabriella," her mom said. "Maybe we can pick out some fun sugar-free gum this weekend."

Gabby smiled, which made the swelling in her face feel strange, which made her laugh . . .

Which made Rico laugh . . .

Which made Mami laugh . . .

Which made Papi laugh. . . .

Gabby was so grateful for her family. Telling the truth *was* a relief.

Gabby woke up Saturday morning feeling guilt-free and ready for fun. She floated into Rico's room and saw her brother attempting a flying kick.

Rico then swirled and twirled and settled into ballet position number five.

"What happened to being a fan of Gum Girl?" Gabby asked with a bittersweet smile.

"I saw Ninja-Rina on TV!" Rico said, breathless, as he leaped out of fifth position to attempt another flying kick.

"You be Gum Girl! I'll be Ninja-Rina!" Rico shouted to Gabby as he continued striking superhero poses.

"Oh!" Gabby said. "Okay, Rico. But you know, anybody can be a hero."

"Anybody?" Rico asked.

"Yep, anybody. Even you!" Gabby laughed and then pretended to be . . . uh . . . *herself!*

The rest of the weekend was gumazing. Gabby and her family went to the park and then they went for *raspados*. Rico ordered a "*tutu* big cup of mango shaved ice." They strolled along the sidewalk eating their *raspados*.

Posters for the city carnival were on every lamppost, every billboard, and every store window. Mrs. Gomez pointed at one of the signs. "*¿Quién quiere ir?* Who wants to go to the carnival?"

ME!

"That's *SUPER*," Mrs. Gomez said, winking at Gabby. "How about we go pick out some *super* sugar-free gum, too?"

Gabby already missed her MIGHTY-MEGA ULTRA-STRETCHY SUPER-DUPER EXTENDA-BUBBLE BUBBLE GUM. But sugar-free gum was way better than no gum at all.

Inside a candy shop, Gabby narrowed her options down to Sugar-Free Strawberry Surge and Sugar-Free Sour Apple Blast. She held a red gumball and a green gumball in front of Rico. "You choose!"

Rico pointed to the big green ball.
Gabby's mouth watered.

CHAPTER 4

A NEW STICKY SITUATION

BACK AT SCHOOL

On Monday morning, Gabby arrived right on time! As she walked to class, Gabby saw Natalie Gooch in the hallway. And she was selling GUM GURL T-shirts?!

Gabby listened in.

. . . we are pretty much best friends now!

"After we stopped the rhino, she took me to her secret Gum Headquarters in her Gum-Mobile! She said that I can drive it anytime!"

A crowd had gathered around Natalie. They wanted to hear more about Robo Chef and the zoo chaos. They also wanted to buy all of Natalie's bootleg GUM GURL T-shirts.

Natalie's stories made Gabby queasy. But Natalie Gooch was not going to ruin another day for Gabby Gomez. She pushed her way past Natalie and the tableful of GUM GURL merchandise. Nothing was going to stop Gabby from getting to class . . . on time!

"Good morning, Ms. Smoot," Gabby said in a cheerful voice.

"Hello, Gabriella," Ms. Smoot said. "I'm glad you're here early. I wanted to talk with you. I've noticed that you've been distracted lately and your grades have dropped."

Gabby's great mood began to fade. With all of her Gum Girl heroic deeds over the past few weeks, she had lost track of her schoolwork!

She tried to smile and think her way out of this new sticky situation.

Ms. Smoot added softly, "But don't worry—it's never too late to make a change. I'll be assigning a new project today. It could help you turn things around."

Ms. Smoot put her hand on Gabby's shoulder and looked her in the eye.

I believe in you, Gabriella!

RRRRING!

The rest of the class rushed in as the bell rang. Everyone was buzzing about Gum Girl *and* the city's newest hero, Ninja-Rina!

"Okay, students, settle down. I have an exciting new project for you," Ms. Smoot said. "And, considering what I've heard, I think you'll like it."

The buzz grew even louder.

"Class, with so many superheroes showing up in town, maybe you'll find some inspiration for our next project."

Ms. Smoot pointed to the board.

"The project is to write an essay about what it means to be a HERO."

¡Aí, no!

CHAPTER 5

HOIST THE FLAG

LATER . . . Ravi Rodriguez, kid reporter, was waiting on the school steps for Gabby.

"I saw your interview on TV," Ravi said.

"Huh?" Gabby said with a gasp. Had Ravi finally figured out her secret identity?

"You know, when Ninja-Rina stopped those thieves from stealing the city sign," Ravi said.

"Oh!" Gabby laughed, remembering her swollen mouth that day. "Could you understand anything I said?"

"Not much. That's why I wanted to ask you—"

Gabby and Ravi looked up to see the school flagpole crashing down!

Gabby panicked. She needed to become Gum Girl right now—in front of Ravi!

But then Ninja-Rina twirled onto the scene.

WHIRL!

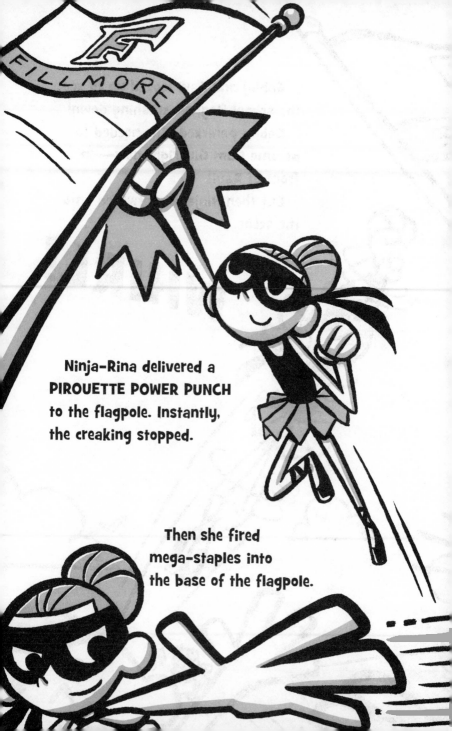

Ninja-Rina delivered a **PIROUETTE POWER PUNCH** to the flagpole. Instantly, the creaking stopped.

Then she fired mega-staples into the base of the flagpole.

Students and teachers cheered! "NINJA . . . RINA!
NINJA . . . RINA!"

A camera crew was already on the scene, luckily.
They captured the whole flagpole rescue and the
chanting crowd of students and teachers. Ravi
dashed toward Ninja-Rina to ask her questions,
while Gabby slipped away as fast as she could.

Who was this new superhero, Gabby wondered on her way home, and where had she come from?

Gabby tried to clear her head and focus on the important thing. *The essay is what matters most. Maybe I'll even have more time to work on it now, thanks to Ninja-Rina.*

Gabby didn't want to waste any time. "Mami," she called as she walked into the house. "Can I work at the library after school this week? We have a big project."

"¡Claro que sí! Of course! I'm glad you are excited. I know you'll do great!"

Gabby smiled.

CHAPTER 6
READY . . .
SET . . .

ACTION!

MEANWHILE . . . Ninja-Rina was EVERYWHERE.

On Tuesday, Ninja-Rina rescued a falling painter.

On Wednesday, Ninja-Rina helped a postal worker being chased by dogs.

On Thursday, Ninja-Rina stopped traffic to let some wandering ducks cross the freeway.

22$
$2

And by Friday, Natalie Gooch was selling
Ninja-Rina-style tutus!

It seemed the whole town was in love with
Ninja-Rina. Had they forgotten about Gum Girl
already?

Gabby walked toward the library to work on her hero essay. On the way, she heard a rustle in the bushes. She peered around to see what was happening.

Ninja-Rina was getting . . . her makeup done?! By her *mom*?! Loaded with trophies and medals, Ninja-Rina's mom was going on and on about how many *more* medals and trophies her daughter would receive.

Gabby looked around. The camera crew was setting up nearby.

Gabby listened carefully. She heard Ninja-Rina telling a masked person exactly *how* to grab a briefcase. "Ready? Okay, let's do it!" Ninja-Rina said.

Just then, the masked person jumped out of the bushes and grabbed a man's briefcase.

Ninja-Rina twirled onto the scene, did a grand
jeté, and then performed a sweeping dropkick
to toss the pretend criminal to the ground. She
handed the briefcase back to its owner.

The crew filmed everything.

CHAPTER 7

NO LUCK & GETTING STUCK

It was time for a Sugar-Free Sour Apple Blast! Gabby reached into her pocket for a bright green gumball. She plopped it into her mouth.

"Whoa!" Gabby winced. "So . . . sour!"

She blew—AGAIN!

The Sour Apple Blast bubble burst!
Gum Girl was back!

Gum Girl dashed over to Ninja-Rina. Gum Girl's feet were *much* less sticky than with regular gum.

I saw everything!

Ninja-Rina leaped into action! Without a warning, she flipped Gum Girl onto her back.

I know jujitsu!

And basket weaving!

It was a whirlwind of Ninja-Rina's vast abilities—all of which she could do with Gum Girl!

Gum Girl was **A LOT** of things right then, but there was one thing she wasn't:

a **quitter.**

Gum Girl pulled herself together and started to spin in a circle. She spun faster . . . and faster . . . and FASTER into a GUM-NADO! She surrounded Ninja-Rina with her warp-speed tornado of gum. "I've got you now!"

But there was one problem: Gum Girl couldn't capture Ninja-Rina! Sugar-Free Sour Apple Blast wasn't sticky enough!

Ninja-Rina hopped left,

then tiptoed right!

Ninja-Rina escaped the gummy whirlwind, grabbed one of her trophies from her ever-present mom, and jammed it into the eye of the storm!

"WHOA!" Gum Girl shouted as she wrapped around and around the trophy. Gum Girl was dizzy, disoriented, and discouraged.

"Now that's a WRAP!" Ninja-Rina said, smiling at the camera.

"And . . . CUT!" a cameraperson yelled.

"That's my cue, Gum Girl. See you next time—and keep the trophy. Ha!"

Ninja-Rina, her mom, and her film crew sped off, leaving Gum Girl dazed and deflated.

CHAPTER 8

GIVE PEACE A CHANCE

Rico watched the news in shock.

City superheroes at odds!

BREAKING NEWS!

Gabby's mouth fell open. Police Chief Lily Yee wanted her to make peace . . . with a fake?! At the carnival? "No way!" Gabby said.

"This is bad," Rico said sadly.

"*No te preocupes.* Don't worry, *hijo*," Dr. Gomez said. "I'm sure Gum Girl and Ninja-Rina will solve their problem."

"No way," Gabby said again.

"Oh, Gabby," Mrs. Gomez chimed in. "I bet they'll show the whole city what it *really* means to be a hero."

Listening to her family talk, something else dawned on Gabby. Something BIG. *They still didn't know she was Gum Girl!*

Gabby thought back to her confession. Papi must have misunderstood her. Now that Gabby thought about it, she realized that *of course* he misunderstood her. Her mouth was numb!

Dr. Gomez turned to Rico. "You'll see, Rico. We'll go to the carnival to watch them resolve things. Okay?"

"Okay, Papi," Rico said.

Okay?! None of this was okay, Gabby thought. *Not in the least.*

Her parents DIDN'T know the truth about her secret identity.

On top of that, Gabby was supposed to make up with that pretend hero, Ninja-Rina, at the city carnival tomorrow night.

AND her essay for Ms. Smoot was due Monday!

If only there was a jar of peanut butter to unstick Gabby from this huge mess.

DUN! DUN! DUN!

CHAPTER 9

TRYING TIMES

Gabby woke up early the next morning to finish her essay for Ms. Smoot. But writing about what it meant to be a hero was the **LAST** thing she felt like doing.

At the library, Gabby tried . . .

And tried . . .

And tried.

It was getting late. Gabby packed up her stuff and headed home, sad and frustrated.

"Ready to go to the carnival?" asked Mrs. Gomez.

"Mami, I don't think I can. I need to finish this essay for Ms. Smoot, otherwise my grades will get even worse!"

Mrs. Gomez understood.

Dr. Gomez gave Gabby a hug. Then they left.

Gabby sat at the kitchen table, staring at her blank report. A blur of pink and black raced past her window. It was Ninja-Rina and her crew. They were off to the city carnival, for sure. And that Fake-o-Rina was probably up to no good!

CHAPTER 10

BIGGEST AND BEST? NOT YET!

The carnival was packed with people. Everyone had come to see Gum Girl and Ninja-Rina.

"Can we go on the Ferris wheel to see the stage better?" Rico asked.

"Great idea!" Dr. Gomez said. "¡Vámonos! Let's go!"

Meanwhile, Police Chief Lily Yee stepped up to the microphone. "Welcome, everyone! Thank you for coming out tonight. We're all excited to see Ninja-Rina and Gum Girl together on this very stage!"

The crowd cheered.

NINJA-RINA! NINJA-RINA! GUM GIRL! GUM GIRL!

Then the mayor whispered something to Police Chief Yee. The crowd quieted to hear the chief. "Unfortunately, I have some bad news. It appears that only Ninja-Rina is here to—"

Suddenly, a flash of green swung onto the stage.

The crowd roared even louder. Gum Girl took her place onstage.

Chief Yee continued, "It appears that Ninja-Rina and Gum Girl are both here!"

Cheers rang out.

"Our city owes an enormous debt of gratitude to BOTH of you fine superheroes," Chief Yee said. "On behalf of all the citizens, I ask: Will you protect and serve our great city *together?*"

Ninja-Rina spun in a perfect pirouette, landing with her hand extended out to Gum Girl. "It would be an honor to serve together," she said.

Gum Girl hesitated. She didn't trust Ninja-Rina. But for the sake of the town, Gum Girl stretched out her hand and shook.

"Thank you!" Chief Yee cheered. "And now, to show our appreciation, the mayor and I would like to offer you this key to the city."

Gum Girl saw Ninja-Rina's mother standing proudly in the front row.

This will be your **BIGGEST** and **BEST** award yet, my little prize!

Chief Yee unrolled a long scroll and began reading. "In recognition of your heroic deeds to keep our city safe, we hereby award this key to the city to both Ninja-Rina and Gum Girl!"

Ninja-Rina and Gum Girl walked side by side toward the microphone. Chief Yee extended the giant golden key.

They both reached for it.

Ninja-Rina pulled.

Gum Girl pulled back. She didn't think someone faking crimes should receive such recognition.

Neither would let go. The more one pulled, the more the other pulled back.

Oh, my!

Hold on! You're TUTU tough to let go!

The crowd watched in silence as the key went back and forth.

Gum Girl pulled left.

Ninja-Rina pulled right.

And then, suddenly, the key flew out of both of their hands. It went up . . . up . . . up!

FLING!

The crowd gasped.

The key started to fall down . . . down . . . down!

It was headed straight for—

—the Ferris wheel!

Oh no! The golden key was jammed into the Ferris wheel gears!
The Ferris wheel

And started to FALL!

DUN! DUN! DUN!

CHAPTER II

FROM TUSSLE TO MUSCLE

Gum Girl watched as the giant Ferris wheel tilted toward the ground. People began screaming.

Police Chief Yee yelled into the microphone, "Help is coming! Don't panic!"

The chief turned to Gum Girl and Ninja-Rina. "We need your help—*both* of you! Can you help them . . . *together?*"

Ninja-Rina looked terrified.

But, but . . . well, I can't . . . I mean, I'm not—

Gum Girl cut her off. "You're strong, Ninja-Rina, and it's going to take two of us to save everyone on that Ferris wheel!"

Come on!

Let's do this!

Gum Girl thought fast. "We've got to anchor the Ferris wheel to the ground. Then we need a bridge to get everyone off."

Ninja-Rina sprang into action, turning Gum Girl into a super-stretchy, extra-springy elastic band. Ninja-Rina spun in a circle and launched Gum Girl into the air.

SWOOSH!

Gum Girl shot straight for a tree. She whipped around the trunk and fired back at Ninja-Rina.

"Got you!" Ninja-Rina called.

"Now to the Ferris wheel!" Gum Girl shouted.

Ninja-Rina spun again, this time flinging Gum Girl toward the top of the Ferris wheel.

FWOOM!

Gum Girl caught a giant spoke. The Ferris wheel came to a stop.

"Everyone, walk down my bridge to safety. Hurry!" she yelled.

Gum Girl suddenly recognized her family at the top of the Ferris wheel.

"¡Ai, no!"

Mrs. Gomez was the first to climb on the Gum Girl bridge.

"You can do it!" Gum Girl said.

Mrs. Gomez took one step. Then another. Then . . . she slipped! Dr. Gomez grabbed her hand and pulled her back on board.

Oh no! The Sugar-Free Sour Apple Blast wasn't sticky enough!

Gum Girl called down to Ninja-Rina. "We need your ninja skills to help people down!"

SLIP!

Ninja-Rina scrambled and flipped up the gummy bridge, jujitsu-style. She held out a hand to Mrs. Gomez.

Mrs. Gomez stepped out again, this time holding Ninja-Rina's hand.

I'll help you!

They quickly
raced to safety.
Then Ninja-Rina
climbed back up.

It was Rico's turn next. He was in the corner trembling, holding on with all his might. "You'll have to jump! I'll catch you," Ninja-Rina called out.

"It's too scary! I can't!" Rico cried.

Dr. Gomez held his son's hand. "It's okay, *hijo*."

You can do it! Anybody can be a hero, Rico!

Rico did a double take and stared at Gum Girl. A flicker of recognition flashed in his eyes. Gum Girl smiled and nodded encouragement.

One . . .

two . . .

THREE!

Rico leaped high into the
air and landed right in Ninja-
Rina's arms.

Mr. Gomez was next,
followed by all of the other
passengers, until only two
remained: Natalie Gooch and
a little boy.

Gum Girl felt her stretchiness fading. She couldn't hold on much longer.

Ninja-Rina reached out to Natalie. But Natalie shrank into the corner of her compartment.

You can do it, Natalie! Grab his hand!

Gum Girl couldn't hold on . . . much . . . longer. . . .

"Please, Natalie! That boy needs you—we all do. We need **YOU**," Ninja-Rina said.

Natalie's eyes brightened. "You need . . . *me?*" Natalie sounded surprised.

"Yes, Natalie. *You!*"

Natalie rose up and reached out her hand to the boy. "I know you're scared. But it's okay."

The little boy smiled. He slowly and cautiously reached out a hand. Natalie grabbed it, then leaped toward Ninja-Rina.

NATALIE GOOCH can save the day!

Just then, Gum Girl's stretchiness failed her.

Gum Girl, Ninja-Rina, Natalie, and the boy spun and spun and spun into the air.

Until they landed in a gummy, gooey mess on the ground.

Everyone was saved!

CHAPTER 12

TRUTH IS THE KEY!

Ravi Rodriguez and a slew of other reporters swarmed Gum Girl and Ninja-Rina.

"Gum Girl, how did you manage to rescue everyone like that?"

Gum Girl laughed and replied, "I only helped. Ninja-Rina is the hero here today." The two heroes smiled at each other, and as Ravi turned to ask Ninja-Rina a question, Gum Girl slipped away and ran into the arms of her family. They were waiting safely away from the crowd.

"Are you guys okay?" she asked.

"Yes, thanks to you," Mrs. Gomez replied.

"Gum Girl, we owe you an apology," Dr. Gomez said. "We were wrong about you—you *saved* us today."

"You want to apologize to *me*?" Gum Girl asked sadly.

"I'm the one who should be apologizing—I haven't been honest with *you*," she continued. Dr. and Mrs. Gomez looked back with confusion. "It's a long story, but I kept chewing gum after you told me not to and then there was this freak accident and I became stretchy. . . ."

Rico gave Gum Girl a giant hug.

Gum Girl stopped trying to explain. Instead, she stretched out her arm to retrieve her backpack with the jar of peanut butter.

She rubbed it on herself and turned back into Gabby Gomez right in front of them!

"It's me, Gabby. I am Gum Girl."

But you . . . ?! Where did you . . . ?! ¿Cómo? How?

"I know it's a lot to take in," Gabby said. "I'm so sorry for keeping this from you. I've been trying to tell you."

Gabby's mom rushed to hug her daughter through her tears. Gabby started crying, too.

Her dad kneeled down and looked Gabby in the eye. "I don't know how you did all of THAT, back there, but that was amazing. You are so brave, *mija*, but the bravest thing you did today was tell the truth."

Gabby smiled and wiped a tear away. She hugged her mom and dad hard.

JUST THEN . . . The Ferris wheel lurched in the distance! What was making the Ferris wheel fall again? Gabby wondered.

SCREECH!

It was Ninja-Rina's mother! She was trying to yank the golden key to the city out of the Ferris wheel.

"I have to go catch that Ferris wheel!" Gabby shouted as she pulled out a Sour Apple Blast gumball.

"Sugar-free?" Dr. Gomez asked.

"Yep!" Gabby popped the gum in her mouth. "That was the deal!" She transformed right in front of them. They were in complete awe.

For the first time, Gum Girl had the *whole* truth on her side, and her family, too. It felt good. She felt like she could do anything!

Gum Girl caught Ninja-Rina's eye, and the two bolted toward Ninja-Rina's mom.

The Ferris wheel crashed into a row of game booths and continued rolling toward a building. Gum Girl chased after it.

Ninja-Rina's mom hung on to the tower by a
single hand, still pulling at the jammed golden key
with the other.

Ninja-Rina climbed up the tower as fast as she
could. "Mom, let the key go! Take my hand!"

Ninja-Rina's mom gasped. She let go of the key and grabbed her daughter's hand instead.

The Ferris wheel tower rocked. It was too late!
It was going to fall straight into the crowd!
Gum Girl stretched one arm to stop the
Ferris wheel and stretched her other arm
to stop the tower from falling. Then she
turned into a gummy net and called
out to Ninja-Rina.

Ninja-Rina, holding on to her mom, pushed off the side of the tower and leaped into the air.
Would they make it?

143

CHAPTER 13

WHAT IT MEANS TO BE A HERO

The next day, Gabby went to the library yet again. This time, she knew exactly what to write for her essay.

When Monday morning rolled around, Gabby handed in her essay to Ms. Smoot.

"Nice work getting this done, Gabriella. I am very excited to read it!" Ms. Smoot said.

Gabby smiled, knowing that what she had written was the truth.

What It Means to Be a Hero
by Gabriella Gomez

Heroes come in all shapes and sizes. They don't have to wear capes or have superpowers. They can be regular people. A hero can be anyone who sees something wrong and tries to fix it. A hero can be a firefighter who rushes into a burning building, or a person who helps someone cross the street. A hero can be a teacher who gives inspiring words to help someone get through a tough time.

Heroes can be two enemies who forgive each other.

A hero can be a person who tells the truth no matter the consequences.

Or a bully who realizes that the world needs her, and does the right thing.

Or someone who knows when to let go.

Being a hero doesn't mean that you don't get scared. It's what you do with the fear. My little brother, Rico, is my hero because he overcame his fears and took a huge leap of faith.

Anybody can be a hero. You need to believe in yourself. But we can never do it all alone; when we take care of each other and do our best, we prove that we all have a hero inside of us!

Gabriella Gomez